Acknowledgments:

There are many people I would like to thank for making this book possible:

Annalise Nawrocki, Zoie, Oren, Miriam, Ari, Sharon and Joseph Hills,
chris and Joanne Nawrocki, Matsue Wiles, Antonio Sacre,
Growing Educators, Maud Hickey, the Los Angeles Percussion Quartet,
Sono Luminus, Michel Marion, Tarah Jeannis, Laurel Tuohy,
cynthia MacGregor, and everyone else at AcutebyDesign.

Lastly, I would like to acknowledge our faithful pooch, Levi--
when you read the book, you'll understand why.
Here's to all of us finding our best friend!

For ZoZo and Mr. Moose

One day, long long ago,
Mother Earth's son was
celebrating his sixth
birthday, and she wanted
to give him the greatest
gift in the entire world.

After talking to
Father Ocean,
Brother Sky,
and Sister Moon,
Mother Earth created
the first bicycle to give to him.

1

The boy was overjoyed.
"This is the best gift ever!
I will always, always keep it with me!"

And for the first month the boy
did just that. He rode the
bicycle everywhere -in
the green forest, down the steep mountain,
and through the rushing river.

3

One day a giant
thunderstorm rained down
from the sky, and the boy
was forced to seek shelter.
He left his bike out in the rain
next to the Great Tree.

4

After the storm was over, the boy raced to
the Great Tree only to find that
his bicycle had disappeared!

The boy cried and cried
until Mother Earth appeared.
"My poor boy," she said, "wipe those
tears away. Remember, nothing is
lost until you've looked everywhere."

"Mother Earth is right," the boy thought.
And so he searched all around the Great Tree until
he found bicycle tracks that led into the green forest.
Delighted, he followed the tracks in
search of his lost bicycle.

At the end of the forest he came upon
Guyde (/guy-day/), the cheetah,
sleeping in the long grass.
"Excuse me, Guyde, have you seen
my bicycle?" asked the boy.

"why yes I have,"
replied Guyde. "I just
rode it in the green forest."

"But I am a cheetah, and I rode the
bicycle so fast that my legs grew tired.
I had to stop for a nap, so I let my friend
Bonate (/bone-ought/), the tortoise,
ride the bicycle down the steep mountain."

8

"Thank you, Guyde," the boy said excitedly,
and he ran off down the steep
mountain in search of Bonate.

9

At the bottom of the mountain
the boy found Bonate relaxing
in the warm sun and eating
some bright green grass.

"Excuse me, Bonate," said the boy,
"Have you seen my bicycle? I left
it out during the storm,
and now it's missing."

"Why yes, I have," responded Bonate.
"I just rode it down the steep mountain."

"But I am a tortoise and I rode the bicycle so slowly that I missed lunch and grew hungry. I had to stop for a snack, so I let my friend Essiamye (/ess-eye-my/), the hippo, ride the bicycle through the rushing river," said the tortoise.

12

"Thank you, Bonate," the boy quickly replied as he hurried off in search of Essiamye. The boy reached the riverbank and carefully swam to the other side, where he found Essiamye enjoying a drink of water.

13

"Excuse...me...Essiamye...,"
the boy said between breaths,
"Have you...seen my...bi...cy...cle?"

"Why yes I have...slurp," said Essiamye,
"I just rode it through the rushing river...slurp."

15

"But I am a large hippo, and I had
such a hard time
balancing on the
bicycle that I
worked up a
huge sweat
...slurp.
I had to stop
to cool off in the river
and, when I came up for air,
the bicycle was gone," said the hippo.

16

The boy
began to cry
for his lost bicycle.
"Thank you...
sniff...
Essiamye...
sniff...," he said.

17

By this time,
the sun was setting,
and the boy decided to
go home and continue
his search the
following day.

"I'll never find my bicycle,"
the boy muttered to himself.
"I went everywhere – in the green forest,
down the steep mountain, and through
the rushing river. It's nowhere,
and I will never find it."

18

when he arrived
home the boy found
Hadye (/hah-duh-yay),
the dog, barking and
jumping up and down.

19

"Hello, Hadye,"
the boy said, sniffling,
"what are you so
excited about today?"
But Hadye could not say.
He was too excited. He just
continued to bark and jump
up and down until the boy
followed him to the
other side of the house.

20

When the boy looked up,
he saw his bicycle.

"Hadye!" the boy exclaimed,
"You found my bicycle and
brought it back to me!
Of all the animals in the
land, you are my best friend!"

22

And to this day,
the dog remains
man's best friend.

AcutebyDesign is a teeny, tiny book publishing
company with a big mission:

To produce and publish high quality diverse,
multicultural, and socially relevant
books for children and young readers
(and occasionally for teachers and parents)

To provide opportunities for teachers and
under-represented writers and illustrators to
publish their dream book, and

To provide small grants to teachers and
parent associations to help provide resources
for underserved students and classrooms.

Thank you for helping to make that dream come true for so many!

www.acutebydesign.com

Percussionist, composer, and storyteller Cory Hills is the creator of "Percussive Storytelling," a program that fuses percussion instruments with oral storytelling, creating exciting sonic worlds for both children and adults. Since 2009, Hills has presented Percussive Storytelling over 350 times to more than 32,000 children in eight countries.

He released his first children's album, *The Lost Bicycle*, in the spring of 2010 and received four national awards, including a gold medal from the NAPPA Parenting Awards, a silver medal from the Parent's Choice Awards, a Preferred Choice from the Creative Child Awards, and World Storytelling Honors. In addition, NAPPA named *The Lost Bicycle* one of the top 13 children's products for 2010.

The success of the album led him to publish his first-ever children's book with AcutebyDesign, so that he could share *The Lost Bicycle* with an even larger audience through words and pictures. The book is a companion piece to *The Lost Bicycle* album, and expands the world and story he created with that recording.

Hills is currently recording a second CD with Sono Luminus Records, due out in early 2016.

He holds degrees from Northwestern University, Queensland Conservatorium, Institute Fabrica, and the University of Kansas.

www.ingramcontent.com/pod-product-compliance
Lightning Source LLC
Chambersburg PA
CBHW042113160726
48295CB00018B/1080